ELI AND THE SWAMP MAN

ELI AND THE SWAMP MAN

CHARLOTTE WATSON SHERMAN

ILLUSTRATED BY JAMES RANSOME

HARPERCOLLINS*PUBLISHERS*

Library of Congress Cataloging-in-Publication Data
Sherman, Charlotte Watson, date
    Eli and the Swamp Man / by Charlotte Watson Sherman ; illustrated by James Ransome.
        p.   cm.
    Summary: Resentful of his stepfather, eight-year-old Eli runs away with a plan to
bike to Alaska to see his father, but a meeting with the mysterious Swamp Man helps
him to change his mind.
    ISBN 0-06-024722-3. — ISBN 0-06-024723-1 (lib. bdg.)
    [1. Stepfathers—Fiction.   2. Remarriage—Fiction.   3. Runaways—Fiction.
4. Afro-Americans—Fiction.]   I. Ransome, James, ill.   II. Title.
PZ7.S54525El   1996   95-39415
[Fic]—dc20   CIP
                                                                                                AC

Typography by Al Cetta
1   2   3   4   5   6   7   8   9   10
❖
First Edition

FOR MY NEPHEWS

CHAPTER ONE

"Eli, let me show you something!"

Eli sat on the floor of his closet in the soft evening light. He pretended he didn't hear his stepfather, Ari, calling him.

J.R., Ari's cat, slowly pushed open Eli's bedroom door with his black nose, stuck his gray head inside the room, and fixed his curious green-eyed gaze on Eli.

"Don't wanna see nuthin' Ari got to show me," Eli whispered fiercely to the cat. J.R. turned slowly, brushed his long gray tail against the closet door, and was gone.

"Crazy cat," Eli muttered as he shuffled his pack of baseball cards. He looked

into the smiling face of Ken Griffey Jr.

"Sure," Eli said, "you can smile. You got a daddy, your same old daddy. I got a stepdaddy who acts like a weirdo."

Eli closed his eyes. In the dark there, he could hear the sound of his daddy playing the harmonica, could feel the notes of their favorite song moving through his body like something free.

*"Camptown races sing that song,
doo-dah, doo-dah,
Camptown races five miles long,
oh doo-dah day . . ."*

"Here, you try," his daddy would say
as he held the cool metal instrument to
Eli's lips. "Block the holes with your
tongue if you want to play just one note.
Then blow hard."

Eli's tongue slopped over the holes in
the harmonica.

"Hold your tongue still," his daddy
laughed.

Eli felt silly, but he blew hard anyway. A thin, wiggly sound flew into the
room and swirled around the ceiling.
He blew again. A second, stronger note
wriggled beside them as they sat on the
floor.

His daddy smiled. Eli closed his eyes

and sucked a sound from one of the little square holes. Eli heard a train whistle blow its sad song.

"Now you got it," his daddy said. "Keep playing."

And Eli pushed his mouth against the cool metal of the harmonica and blew and sucked, fast notes and slow ones, high sounds and low. Eli played his daddy's harmonica as if his rickety music could keep his father sitting on the floor of his room, next to his messy bed, beside him, forever.

But that was before his daddy had left their red house on the hill in Seattle three years ago with his suitcases full. Before his daddy had waved good-bye to him and his sister, Savannah, and boarded the airplane to Alaska. Before his mama and daddy had sadly told him and Savannah about the divorce.

He had felt as if a world had split open inside him. He didn't say much about it, though. Now he wished he had. Maybe he could have stopped it and his mama wouldn't have married Ari.

Eli opened his eyes as Savannah walked into his room. Even though she was ten years old and only two years older than him, Savannah thought she knew so much. She bent over and kicked her legs into the air until she was standing on her hands in front of the closet. People always said she looked just like Mama, only shorter. The gold beads in Savannah's cornrows gleamed in the fading light of the room as they dangled and clacked against the floor.

"You hear Ari calling you?" she asked sharply.

Savannah liked Ari. She liked paddling in the canoe around the shores of

Lake Washington with Mama and Ari as she pretended to be some old warrior queen. "I'm an Indian princess," she always said after they came home from a canoeing trip. "And I'm Superman," Eli would yell as he ran into his room and slammed the door. Eli hated canoeing. He knew he was strong enough to hold the paddle, but pulling it through the heavy water always made his spidery arms ache.

"I hear," he said glumly. "I don't wanna go."

"He wants to show you how he sews those beads on his costume. I helped some. You better come like he asked."

"He ain't getting me sewing," Eli said. "Besides, I don't wanna go on no vacation with him. I don't wanna go to New Orleans. It ain't fair."

"It isn't fair. Not ain't. You better be

glad you get to go anyplace. Mardi Gras sounds like fun to me."

"Well, I ain't going," Eli said, folding his arms across his chest. "I'm gonna find a way to go see Daddy in Alaska, you watch."

"You gonna find a way to get in *big trouble.* Daddy didn't say anything about you going to see him in Alaska," Savannah said as she dropped her legs to the ground and cartwheeled out of the room.

"Miss Know-It-All Savannah makes me sick," Eli thought. "I don't have to wait for Daddy to tell me to come to Alaska. I can go see him anytime I get ready."

Eli frowned, then stood and stretched in the closet. He couldn't see his baseball cards anymore. He stepped outside the closet into the darkness of his room. The white eye of the rising moon peeped through the window. He left his room to see what Ari wanted to show him. "Maybe then he'll leave me alone," he thought.

Eli had never wanted his daddy to leave him alone. He could go fishing with his daddy and sit with him for hours on the dock and listen to his daddy tell stories and jokes.

"Why didn't the skeleton ask his girl-friend to the dance?"

"I don't know. Why?" Eli had asked.

"Because he didn't have any guts," his daddy had said, laughing as hard as Eli.

Eli didn't like Ari's jokes. Once, Ari interrupted Eli as he watched a baseball game on television to tell him a joke.

"Why did the ghost starch his sheet?"

"What?" Eli asked as Ken Griffey Jr. stepped up to the plate to bat.

"Why did the ghost starch his sheet?"

"I don't know," Eli said.

"Because he was scared stiff," Ari said, then waited for Eli to laugh.

Eli did not think the joke was funny. But even worse was the fact that he had missed Ken Griffey Jr.'s second home run of the game, listening to Ari's dumb joke.

There Ari was, sitting at the kitchen table, not even tilting the wooden chair on its hind legs and rocking, like Daddy liked to do.

Eli could hear Savannah and her friends, those giggly twins, Ayesha and Zahida, playing ring-around-the-rosy in the living room. The twins had swirly dresses on, and the beads in their hair clicked as they spun like a world in the center of the room.

Eli's mama, Ruby, sat beside Ari smiling. She was lightly stroking his arm.

She looked at Ari like suns and moons were in her eyes. Seashells and blue-black stars. It made Eli feel funny inside when Mama looked at Ari like that.

"That's how she used to look at Daddy before he went away," Eli thought. "That's how she looks at me and Savannah. With happy eyes." Eli didn't like his mama to look at Ari that way.

"Why does she like him?" Eli wondered. "What kind of man goes around in pants like that?" Eli asked under his breath as he looked beneath the table and saw the thirty-one-flavor-ice-cream–colored, wide-legged balloon pants Ari liked to wear. "What kind of man wears clown pants when he's not a clown?"

"Eli, I want you to see this," Ari said proudly. "I'm going to mask Indian this year in New Orleans." He handed Eli a square of cloth covered with tiny rainbow-colored beads.

"I'm going to sew all these squares into my costume."

Eli took the cloth and stared. A box overflowing with cloth sat on the floor beside Ari. A frown crinkled Eli's face.

"Right," Eli said to himself. "Masking Indian. Where a bunch of men dress up like old-time Indian chiefs and pretend to have a word war."

Ari looked as if he could read Eli's mind.

"There's a history to this celebration, Eli. It's not just a bunch of guys dressing up and acting silly."

Oh, no. He could feel Ari warming up for another history lesson now. And Mama wasn't going to stop him, either. Eli wanted to lie on the wood floor and throw the cloth over his face like a beaded shield that had the power to hold back all the words that were beginning to fall from Ari's mouth like bullets of air.

Eli scowled as Savannah, Ayesha, and Zahida ran into the kitchen and sat on the floor at Ari's feet. They weren't even acting giggly or silly, like they were moments ago.

"Many African slaves ran away from plantations and met Indians who let them live with them in the hills, mountains, swamps, and woods," Ari began.

"I bet some of those runaways were kids, just like me," Eli said.

"You're absolutely right, Eli," Ari said eagerly. "Some of the runaways were kids. Some ran away with their parents and some ran away by themselves. Some went north to Canada and some stayed South and lived with the Seminole Nation. The name Seminole means runaways, and two of their leaders, Chief Osceola and his son, Wild Cat, fought the United States Army to protect their land and to help keep the African runaways free."

"We mask Indian to thank those Indians who helped our ancestors, those runaway Africans," Mama said, and Ari nodded. It made Eli mad to see them nodding in agreement, as one.

"Do you think some of them are still there, waiting to help people in the woods?" Eli asked.

"What a dumb question, Eli!" Savannah said.

"No, Savannah. There are no dumb questions," Ari said. He turned and gently placed his hand on Eli's shoulder.

"I don't know if any of those helpers are living in the woods today. But I like to believe they are," Ari said.

"We can see when we get to New

Orleans!" Savannah whooped. "We'll walk behind a big chief to the park at the center of town. The chiefs work on their costumes for a year before they're ready, don't they, Mama?"

Mama nodded, smiling. Eli looked from Ari to Mama to Savannah. They were all happy about the upcoming trip.

"They use eggshells, seashells, broken glass, ribbons," Savannah continued happily. "Rhinestones, fish scales, glass beads, sequins. Ostrich, peacock, and turkey feathers.

"As they sew, they sing:

'Sew! Sew! Sew!
Shoo Katy way, hi-ko
Somebody gotta sew, sew, sew . . .' "

"They paint their faces to look like warriors," Mama chimed in. "Some hold feathered sticks, pipes, hatchets, and skulls in their hands."

"When all the big chiefs get to the park, the war of words begins," Savannah said. "They chant and dance, praising the Indian tribes they've chosen to honor. At the end of the day, the chief with the best costume—and quickest tongue—is declared the winner."

Savannah finally stopped talking and began to dance in a circle around Ari's chair.

Ari jumped up from his chair and started chanting and dancing.

"Baba eh oh, me babalayo, obatala, eh oh . . ." he sang. "Come dance with me, Eli. I'll teach you a Seminole stomp dance. We'll sew a costume for you, too."

"I ain't dancing with you," Eli thought. "But I am gonna run away from here

just like those runaway Africans and go live with my daddy."

Eli threw the beaded cloth on the kitchen table, ignored the sad look on Mama's face, and stomped to his bedroom. He plugged his ears when he later heard Mama and Ari dancing around the room.

CHAPTER TWO

When Eli woke the next morning, he lay inside his rumpled sheets and began to plan how he would run away. He stared at the postcard of Cordova, Alaska, that hung on the wall beside his bed.

His daddy had sent him the card when Eli was six, one year after the divorce. A small knot tightened inside Eli's stomach as he slowly counted how long it had been since he had seen his daddy. One, two, three years since his daddy had moved to Cordova.

Eli's eyes began to burn, but J.R. was

the only one who saw his tears. He watched his tears darken the fur on J.R.'s back.

Eli looked at the postcard with watery eyes. Cordova looked like a wild place. A forest surrounded the base of a purple-skinned mountain covered with snow. Trees with leaves as big as Eli's head nearly touched the sky with their tips. The head of a bald eagle shone white against the dark mountain as it stretched its huge, light wings and soared gently through the air.

A bushy place. A magic place. His daddy's home.

Eli would go there. He would ride his bike as far north as he could go. When he couldn't travel any farther by land, he'd catch a ride on a fishing boat and sail the rest of the way.

His daddy would be glad to see him.

If he left quickly and quietly, Mama and Ari wouldn't even have to know he had gone.

Eli got up and put his swimming trunks and baseball cards into a small pile on his bed. He would pack them into the saddlebags on his bike after he made himself a peanut-butter-and-pickle sandwich.

He found a picture inside his drawer of him and his daddy, Mama, and Savannah in the happy days before the divorce. He felt a small sun burning inside his chest when he looked at that picture. At least Ari wasn't in it. He hadn't come into their lives and married Mama until two years after the divorce.

Eli decided to pack the picture in his saddlebag too.

He didn't want to say good-bye to Savannah. He knew she would try to make him change his mind about running away. But he did want to say good-bye to Mama.

She was sitting in the kitchen with Ari. From the sweet smell in the air, Eli knew Ari was making blueberry pancakes, Eli's favorite.

"Ready for pancakes, Eli?" Ari asked.

Eli thought for a minute. He kicked the floor with the toe of his tennis shoe. If he ate the pancakes, it would take him that much longer to get to Alaska.

"I ain't hungry," Eli said.

"I'm not hungry," Savannah said, cartwheeling through the kitchen. "Not ain't."

"I ain't talking to you," Eli said grumpily. Savannah stopped turning like a wheel in the room and stood on her hands with her back against the wall.

"I'm not talking to you, egghead," she

said, talking upside-down.

"Good," Eli said. He gave Mama a fast kiss on the cheek. She looked at him with worried eyes. Eli felt his stomach scrunch at the thought of leaving her, but he knew he had to go. He decided to leave without the sandwich.

"Where are you off to in such a hurry?" Mama asked.

"Me and Jeffre and Talen are gonna ride bikes and stuff," Eli said uneasily.

He didn't like telling a lie to Mama. "See you," he said. He went upstairs to pack his saddlebags.

Eli wondered if he could get his best friends, Antoine, Talen, and Jeffre, to go with him to Alaska. If they came, they would have fun riding their bikes through the mountains and fishing in the rivers they would pass. Maybe they would see a cougar, or a bear.

But Eli worried if his friends would understand his wanting to leave home and go live with his daddy in Alaska. They all liked Ari.

Once, Ari had dressed them up in his old Mardi Gras costumes.

"Antoine, you be the witch doctor," Ari had said as he placed a necklace with shells and small bones around Antoine's neck. "And this is a healing stick. It's for making the sick well." Ari handed him a stick with red and gold feathers tied to its tip.

Next, Ari scooped his hand in a small pot of white gunk and smeared it on Talen's face. He painted three white stripes on each of Talen's cheeks. Ari scooped more gunk out of another small pot and painted one red stripe on Talen's forehead, over his nose, across his lips, and down to his chin.

"You are now a griot, the village storyteller. You'll keep track of everything that happens to all the people of this village and tell us stories that make us laugh and cry."

Then Ari let the boys touch a long beaded belt he held in his hands. The belt had a black snake, an orange sun, and purple stars on it. Ari swung the belt in the air. Then he wrapped it around

Jeffre's waist. He had to wrap it around Jeffre's waist four times because it was so big.

"This is the warrior belt, Jeffre. Only the strongest, bravest boys are allowed to wear this belt."

Eli looked at his three best friends. They looked like they liked all the weird stuff Ari was saying. They looked like they believed it. The proud looks on their faces made Eli mad. Whose friends were they anyway, his or Ari's? He turned to walk away.

"Wait, Eli. This headdress is for you. It's for the big chief," Ari had called out, but Eli was moving so fast, he didn't hear the rest of what Ari had to say.

If his daddy were here, he'd show Ari how to really make things fun. If his friends got a chance to play the harmonica or go fishing with his daddy, they would like him better than Ari too. Eli knew they would.

Eli decided to stop at Antoine's house and ask him to come to Cordova.

"Antoine home?" he asked Antoine's sister, Rose. Rose didn't look like a flower, and she smelled like the gymnasium at school. She was on the same gymnastics team as Savannah.

"He's out back with Tuffy," she said. Then she blew a big bubble-gum bubble in Eli's face.

Eli got to the backyard just in time. Antoine was placing his turtle, Tuffy, in a shallow hole in the ground.

"He died last night. Just stopped breathing. My dad said he must've caught some turtle disease," Antoine said. His eyes were puffy and red. Once, Antoine had brought Tuffy to school so he could race a fifth grader's turtle across the lunchroom floor. Tuffy hadn't won the race.

Eli helped Antoine fill the hole. They pushed the soft dark dirt into a small mound on top of the hole. Antoine stood a little twig in the mound like a flag.

"So we can remember where he is. Like Grandpa," he said quietly. The boys didn't speak for a minute.

Then Eli asked, "You want to ride bikes with me to Alaska?"

"I thought you and your mama and Ari and Savannah was going to New Orleans," Antoine said.

"Naw," Eli said. "I'm going to see my daddy in Cordova."

"Alaska's a long way from here," Antoine said, scratching his nose. "It'll take you a month to get there."

"I'm gonna ride my bike. It won't

take long," Eli said. "I'm gonna ride fast."

"You gonna ride fast enough to get all the way up there before school starts? 'Cause I'd have to be back by then."

"I'm gonna do it. You wanna come?" Eli asked.

"Nope. You gonna have to ride faster than a airplane. Anyway, I gotta help my dad cut the grass today. If I go to Alaska with you, I won't be back in time," Antoine said.

Disappointment made Eli's shoulders sink. Antoine was his bravest friend. He wasn't even scared of Nashad Thompkins, that freckle-faced fifth grader who liked to make the third- and fourth-grade boys arm-wrestle him whether they wanted to or not. Nashad always won, but one time Antoine almost beat him.

If they had to fight a bear on the way to

Alaska, Eli had been counting on Antoine to be by his side.

"You sure you don't wanna come?" Eli asked.

Antoine nodded.

"Well, I gotta go. Sorry about Tuffy," Eli said.

"Wait. Let me get something for you to take with you."

Eli stood by Tuffy's grave while Antoine ran inside the house. He came back a few minutes later.

"Here," he said, handing his favorite black marble to Eli. It had squiggly lines scratched around its sides. It looked big as a bear's eye. "For good luck," Antoine said.

Eli remembered Antoine had had the lucky marble in his pocket the day Tuffy lost the race at school. He was glad to have it anyway, though.

"Thanks," Eli said.

"When you coming back?" Antoine asked.

"I dunno," Eli said.

The boys shook hands. Eli waved as he left the backyard.

li rode his bike four blocks to Talen's house.

Talen lived with his grandmother, Miz Ollie. Some kids thought Miz Ollie was a witch. Talen said she wasn't.

She was short and had wild black hair with a white spot in the back of her head. She wore long skirts and silver bracelets that jingled when she walked. She smelled like a pinecone. Sometimes she played her piano like lightning was inside her fingers as they moved across the black and white keys, making music. Witch music.

Miz Ollie opened the door before Eli could knock. He gulped. He was a little bit scared of Miz Ollie and had hoped she wouldn't be home. She looked into his eyes. Eli blinked three quick times. Miz Ollie had one brown eye and one green eye. He wondered if she could read his mind, like witches are supposed to be able to do.

"Talen gone," Miz Ollie said in a scratchy voice. "Come sit with me till he come home." She pulled Eli inside the house before he could say no.

"I . . . I . . ." was all Eli said. He didn't want to sit with Miz Ollie.

"He at the store. Be back in a minute. You ready to go to New Orleans?" she asked. Everybody knew about Ari's dumb trip.

"No, ma'am. I mean, yes ma'am," Eli said nervously.

"I don't think you ready," she said.

Miz Ollie reached for Eli. He tried not to jump away. The long red tips of her fingers scratched his arm as she tried to grab his sweaty hand. He couldn't move.

"You like Talen's old uncle Wishbone," she said. "Hardheaded. Can't see what you got right in your hands, always wishing on something ain't never gonna be."

Eli looked at Miz Ollie's teeth while she talked. They were straight and white and pointy. Witch teeth.

"I ain't wishing for nuthin'," Eli whispered.

"There's a wishing place in you big as the world. We's all got one. Sometimes what we wishing for is right there, but we think it's over some yonder place."

"I . . . I . . . I don't know . . ." Eli started to say, but then Talen opened the door and let light inside the dim front room.

"Hey," Talen said.

"Hey," Eli said, relieved to follow Talen up the long dark stairs to his room.

"Be careful on your trip," Miz Ollie called after Eli in her scratchiest voice.

Eli turned to stare at Miz Ollie. She watched him with her brown eye closed. Her green eye was lit up inside. She looked straight through Eli for a long moment.

"She knows what I'm going to do," Eli thought. He turned and quickly followed Talen before she could put one of her spells on him.

Eli wondered if Talen liked living with a witch.

"Had to get glue for my boat," Talen said.

Eli picked up the boat made out of

Popsicle sticks. It had a square sail made out of stiff white cloth.

"You wanna come with me to Alaska?" Eli asked.

"What you going to Alaska for?" Talen asked.

"To be with my daddy," Eli said.

"Oh," Talen said. He couldn't be with his mama or daddy 'cause they both got killed in a car crash.

"You gonna leave your mama and Savannah and Ari? You gonna leave your family?" Talen asked. Talen always said it made him sad that he couldn't remember what his mama's and daddy's voices sounded like.

Eli nodded his head. He closed his eyes and inhaled deeply. He smelled his mama's smell, saffron. He opened his eyes. Now Ari smelled like that too.

"Ari ain't my family," Eli said. "Always

acting like he knows how to be somebody's daddy. Trying to teach me that
stupid karate stuff and going up to the
school talking to my teachers with Mama.
He ain't my daddy. He can't even play
no harmonica and he don't like to fish.
He don't know nothing."

"Ari seem all right to me," Talen said.

"That's 'cause you don't have to live
with him. Now he wants us all to go to
New Orleans. Somewhere I don't never
want to go. The only place I wanna go is
to see my daddy. Not to no New Orleans
with him," Eli said.

"I like it when he tries to teach us
stuff," Talen said. "I wish I had a daddy.
Even one like Ari."

"Yeah, 'cause you got a grandma
that's a witch," Eli thought. "Anything
okay with you after her."

"You coming?" Eli asked.

"I can't leave my grandma. She needs me here. I got something for you to take with you, though," Talen said. He pulled out drawer after messy drawer till he found what he was looking for.

He handed Eli an old faded blanket.

"That's my Jammo," he said. "My uncle Wishbone gave it to me after my mama and daddy got killed. Wishbone said they wasn't never coming back, but I could hold on to this Jammo and it'd

be like I was holding them. You can sleep with it at night on your trip. Won't nuthin' bother you at night with Jammo."

"Thanks," Eli said, holding the musty-smelling blanket.

"Be careful," Talen said, punching Eli in the arm.

"See you," Eli said as he quickly ran down the steps to get to his bike before Miz Ollie could say anything else to him.

CHAPTER FOUR

Slowly Eli rode to Jeffre's house. It was almost noon and he was tired and hungry after pedaling to the top of the hill. Eli saw Jeffre sitting on his porch, sucking his thumb. Sometimes his mama put hot sauce on his thumb to try to make him stop sucking it, but he still wouldn't stop.

"You wanna ride with me to my daddy's house in Alaska?" Eli asked.

"That's a trillion miles from here," Jeffre said, pulling his thumb out of his mouth.

"I'm gonna ride fast," Eli said.

"You know the way?" Jeffre asked.

"It's like going to the North Pole," Eli said. "I'm gonna ride north."

"You gonna ride past Mount Rainier?"

"Naw, that's the wrong way. I gotta follow the North Star."

"Bet you'll get there faster if you go through the swamp," Jeffre said. "But watch out for the Swamp Man." He sucked his thumb again.

Everybody was scared of the Swamp Man. Eli saw him once when he was catching tadpoles in a jar down in the swamp. The Swamp Man was stooping under the old green bridge, watching. A shadow covered his face.

The shabby green coat he wore didn't have sleeves. It was torn and tattered, and hung to the ground. On his hands were old dirty gloves with holes in the tips. He held his hand up slow, and waved. Eli jumped, turned, and dropped his jar of tadpoles into the swamp's slick green water. Then Eli ran away.

Antoine's cousin, Cheese, said the Swamp Man had big square teeth that he used to bite the ears off kids he caught playing in the woods.

Walter Calhoun said the Swamp Man tried to grab him one day and pull him up into the trees.

Savannah liked to talk about the time she went with Ayesha and Zahida to the swamp. They went to catch salamanders but didn't get a chance to catch any that day. Once they got to the bridge that crossed the swamp, they stopped walking and they all screamed. On the floor of the bridge lay a pair of false teeth, big clacking square yellow teeth with pink pink gums.

The Swamp Man climbed from beneath the bridge and stood before the three shaking girls. Then he bowed to them. Savannah said his head was bald as an egg. When he stood straight and tall before them again, he grinned. Savannah said there were no teeth in his mouth. The girls yelled as if he were a ghost and not a flesh-and-blood man. They ran as fast as their legs would carry them.

"Wanna come with me?" Eli asked Jeffre again. As much as he wanted to get to Alaska and his daddy, he did not want to ride through the woods alone. Hungry and alone.

Jeffre looked at the sky, the blue bowl of the sky. Cotton-candy clouds were overhead. A bluebird cheeped in an evergreen tree.

"Naw," Jeffre said.

"You scared?" Eli asked.

"You ain't?" Jeffre asked.

"The Swamp Man don't scare me," Eli said.

"He don't scare me, neither, but I ain't going nowhere where I might see him. I'm gonna go down to the park after while and play some ball. You wanna come?"

"If I play ball with you, it'll take me longer to get to Alaska," Eli said.

"Well, I guess I'll see you when you

get back, then," Jeffre said. "Talen told me the Swamp Man is worse than a witch. He'll catch you and put you in a fire, then he'll do a three little pigs jig while he's cooking you."

"I guess I'll see you later, then," Eli said sadly.

"Wait," Jeffre said. "Madison'll go with you." He went into the house, and returned holding a silver coffee can in his hands.

"You'll have to get him some worms along the way," Jeffre said. He pressed the can into Eli's hands.

Inside lay Madison, Jeffre's orange-and-black-spotted salamander. He had yellow-toed feet.

"Madison'll keep the Swamp Man away," Jeffre said. "He's not scared of anybody."

Eli gripped the cool can tightly.

"Told you I ain't scared of no Swamp Man," he said, though he was glad to have some company on his trip, even if it was a salamander. Now he wouldn't feel so alone.

"Thanks," Eli said. He thumped Jeffre's thumb.

"You welcome," Jeffre said. He stuck his thumb back inside his mouth and sucked while Eli packed Madison's can inside a saddlebag. He waved as Eli rode down the hill toward the trees and the swamp.

CHAPTER FIVE

Eli pedaled furiously toward the swamp. He tried to push the little seed of disappointment growing inside his belly into the wind blowing beneath his circling feet. He had been sure Antoine would join him on this trip. Antoine loved adventures and secrets and scary things. He would walk right up to the Swamp Man and talk to him, maybe even shake his hand. No matter what stories Talen and Jeffre had told about the man.

Alaska was going to be a long ride without any of his friends beside him.

Antoine's marble and the can holding

Jeffre's salamander, Madison, clanked inside his saddlebag and made a rickety song.

Though his legs were beginning to ache, Eli kept pumping his pedals as fast as he could.

Should he really try to ride to Alaska? He already missed the warmth of Mama's arms holding him. The way her slender fingers stroked his face when he sat in her lap the times he felt scared or sad or so so alone with his daddy gone.

It had already been hours since Miss Know-It-All Savannah had tried to tell him what to do. Who would go with her to the woods to look for tree frogs now that he had gone? She would probably try to kill him half to death for leaving.

What if he never saw Mama or Savannah again?

Eli slowed his bike as his eyes began

to fill with water. This was all Ari's fault anyway. If only his mother had never married him, Eli wouldn't be running away. If only his daddy still lived in their house . . .

Eli couldn't wait to see his father. Would they go fishing first or mountain climbing? Maybe they'd go hunting for a bear.

A tiny flame of doubt flickered inside Eli's mind. For the first time in a long while, he let himself remember the last picture his daddy had mailed him and Savannah. The picture of his new wife and their baby boy.

The woman his daddy said he had married had a crinkly smile and curly hair all over her head. Her name was Angela. The baby's name was Nathan. Eli thought he looked like a grinch. How could his daddy look so happy in that picture? Eli hadn't seen him smile like that in a long, long time.

Did his daddy play the harmonica for Nathan, too? What if he didn't want Eli anymore now that he had this new baby boy? He hadn't written Eli or Savannah in months. Eli hadn't seen him for three years, since he moved to Alaska. Maybe his daddy had changed. Maybe he didn't even play the harmonica anymore.

Eli decided to stop thinking about his daddy for now. He shook the sad thoughts about him out of his head. He dried his eyes and wiped his face with his shirtsleeve.

Soon he neared the trees that led to the swamp. He cut through the patch of ponderosa pines that lined the worn trail and slowed his bike once more.

The trees blocked the sun's warm fingers of light. Eli shivered as he rode toward a clearing deep in the woods. He stopped his bike and rested at the top of a gravelly hill.

There at the bottom of the hill lay the footbridge that crossed the green waters of the swamp. The bridge he had to cross to get to Alaska. The Swamp Man's bridge. Eli felt his stomach start to smoosh like it always did when he was afraid.

Eli coasted down the hill, slowly picking up speed.

Eli closed his eyes for a second. He felt as if he were flying. Flying toward his daddy and his new home.

Thonk.

Too late, Eli opened his eyes. His front wheel had hit a large rock, and the bike twisted to the left. Eli lost his grip on the handlebars and flew to the right. He yelled as he fell to the ground.

Eli lay spread-eagled on the damp earth. He heard the wind moving soft as a prayer through the tall skinny grass that grew around the bank of the swamp. The air smelled like dry leaves and rotten eggs and the promise of a warm green summer. He heard a choir of crickets nearby.

Eli slowly pulled himself to his knees. He saw a hollow tree lying on the ground not far from where he crouched.

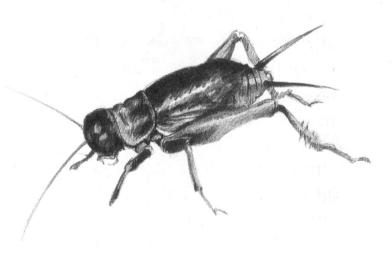

He crawled to the tree and settled himself against it. The wind was singing a sweet murmuring song and the tree held him gently, safely. He heard leaves crackling nearby. Something was moving through the woods toward him.

Eli turned his head toward the sound. He jumped. From the edge of the stand of trees Eli saw red-streaked eyes looking at him. He was looking into the large eyes of the Swamp Man.

Eli didn't know which way to get up and run. His bike lay on the ground too far away for him to get to it quickly. The swamp lay behind him; trees surrounded him. All directions led straight to the Swamp Man.

The Swamp Man laughed. It was a wild sound, loud and long.

"You all right?" the Swamp Man finally asked as he walked toward Eli, holding an outstretched dirty-gloved hand to help Eli to his feet.

The Swamp Man's fingertips were rough and wide. Eli shakily stood.

Eli nodded slowly. He felt the thump-thumping of his heart loudly beneath his shirt. He swallowed a lump as big as a lemon inside his throat. He had never been this close to the Swamp Man.

The Swamp Man smelled like the swamp. His pants looked two sizes too big, and there were large holes in the knees. Eli could see another pair of pants beneath the top pair.

The Swamp Man watched Eli look him over for a moment before he pointed toward Eli's bike.

"Look like you took a pretty bad fall, boy. You sure you all right?" he asked.

For a moment Eli didn't respond. Maybe the Swamp Man's questions were

a trick. Maybe he was being nice so he could get up close and bite Eli's ears with his big teeth.

When the Swamp Man didn't make a move to grab Eli with his long arms and bite him or fly with him to the top of the trees, Eli said, "I'm all right."

"You better check your bike, then," the Swamp Man said.

Eli glanced toward the Swamp Man's outstretched fingers.

"Oh, no," he cried. His saddlebag was open and Madison's coffee can lay on the ground. Eli ran and picked it up. It was empty. Even the few strands of grass Jeffre had put inside for Madison to lie on were gone.

Eli looked around him. Trees as tall as mountains everywhere. Ferns and long-legged grass covered the ground. The swamp lay in front of Eli, the Swamp

Man stood behind him. Madison could be anywhere.

Eli ran to the edge of the swamp. The Swamp Man slowly followed.

The green water of the swamp moved sluggishly, filled with life. Skinny dark shadows darted beneath its surface. Dragonflies moved across the water like thin blue flames. Madison was nowhere to be seen.

"What was in the can?" the Swamp Man asked kindly.

Eli jumped. For a moment he had forgotten the Swamp Man.

"Madison, my friend's salamander," Eli said sadly.

"He come when you call?" the Swamp Man asked.

"No," Eli said. He hadn't ever seen Madison come to Jeffre when he called him. He just sat on his rock.

Eli bit his lower lip.

"We can find him," the Swamp Man said. "Stay out here till we do. I know what it's like to lose something important to you. I lost plenty important things," the Swamp Man muttered as he walked toward the bridge that crossed the swamp.

Eli looked at the Swamp Man's tattered coat and scrunched-up hat. He wondered what important things the Swamp Man had lost.

"Where you headed?" asked the Swamp Man.

"Going to Alaska," Eli said as he joined the Swamp Man and walked along the edge of the swamp.

The Swamp Man looked at Eli strangely.

"This my swamp. You wanna pass through here, you gotta go by me," the Swamp Man said.

Eli took a deep breath. He smelled pinecones and swamp muck. His arms and legs felt as if he had already wrestled the Swamp Man and lost. His stomach grumbled. "Your big stomach just ate your little stomach," his daddy used to say to him when he heard Eli's empty belly growl.

Eli was so tired and hungry, he knew that if the Swamp Man wanted to fight him now, he would beat Eli with both hands tied behind his tattered back. But Eli had no choice but to follow him, follow the Swamp Man wherever he might go.

Eli and the Swamp Man walked along the bank of the swamp, calling for Madison. The Swamp Man dipped when he walked, like one leg was shorter than the other. Sometimes he stopped, put his holey glove to his mouth, and whistled like he was calling the birds twittering in the branches.

Eli looked at the strange shapes the twisted trees made in the dark light. Murmuring whispers whooshed from the shadows. Eli's feet sank into the oozing mud; they couldn't plant themselves in the mucky ground.

The Swamp Man didn't look so scary stooped down poking the tips of his fingers into the water with his gloves on, calling, "Maddie's son, Maddie's son."

"His name's Madison," Eli said after a while. It always made Eli mad when people said his name wrong, especially when they called him "Ellie."

"His mama named Maddie?" the Swamp Man asked.

"Don't know," Eli said. His eyes scanned the green water for Madison. Ari would've asked Eli something like that. Something dumb, that he thought was funny. Maybe all grown-ups asked dumb questions. Eli looked steadily into the Swamp Man's face for the first time without fear.

"Oh. I thought that's why you called him Maddie's son, get it?" he asked, and then he laughed that wild laugh again.

For a minute Eli was afraid. Then he laughed too. He pulled his feet out of the mud and made his way toward firmer ground.

"He's not mine. He's my friend Jeffre's," Eli said.

"What you doing with him?" the Swamp Man asked.

"Taking him with me to Alaska," Eli said.

"Why you going there?" the Swamp Man asked.

Eli thought for a minute. Should he tell the Swamp Man about his daddy who used to take him fishing? Just him and his daddy in the rowboat in the middle of the lake, sitting, laughing, being still on top of water calm and clear as blue ice?

And Savannah? Should he tell the Swamp Man about the way they used to get under the covers of Savannah's bed with a flashlight while she read stories that made him shiver even though it was hot under the blankets? But he wouldn't let Savannah stop reading until the scariest parts were over and he didn't see a monster when he stuck his head out of the covers to run back to his room.

Would the Swamp Man understand if he told him about Mama and the way she makes the kitchen smell when she bakes her sweet-potato pies and how her hugs are better then pie, better than even his most favorite baseball cards?

Should he tell him about the funny way his stomach scrunches when Mama looks at Ari?

"My daddy's there" was all he said.

"You ain't got no other people?" the Swamp Man asked.

"Yeah," Eli said.

"Who?"

"My sister . . . and my mama and my stepfather, Ari," Eli finally said.

"I see," the Swamp Man said.

Eli walked over to the Swamp Man. He stuck his fingers into the murky green water of the swamp. It was cold and slimy. And it didn't smell good. He pressed his fingers into the swamp bank's muck. He wasn't ever going to find Madison if he was in there.

The Swamp Man stood. "What else you bring with you?" he asked, pointing the round toe of his big muddy boot in the direction of Eli's bike.

Eli ran to his bike. He stooped and pulled out his baseball cards, swimming trunks, and the picture of him, his daddy, Mama, and Savannah. He even pulled out Talen's Jammo.

"Look like you ready for a long trip,"

the Swamp Man said, standing beside him.

"Yeah," was all Eli said.

"I been living out here awhile, boy, and there's all kind of things I got to do for myself. I don't got no mama or sister, or no daddy to do for me. Sound like you got two daddies and I bet you don't like one of 'em."

"Ari wants me to go to New Orleans and celebrate some old Indian stuff with him."

"Indian stuff?"

"Those old Indians that helped the runaway slaves. He wants to dance around and whoop and holler."

"Your stepdaddy mask Indian?" The Swamp Man started to smile.

Eli nodded slowly.

"Then he all right with me. I masked Indian once or twice before myself.

That's where I'm from. New Orleans. Louisiana. You ain't lived till you tasted some Louisiana crawfish. You ever had any?"

Eli shook his head no.

"They just little lobsters. You crack 'em in half, suck the heads, and eat the tails. Good eating."

Eli knew he didn't want to suck the heads of any crawfish. Anyway, he was not going to go to New Orleans.

"And they got real swamps there. Nothing like this little creek. Got black grasshoppers big as my hand. You ever seen a alligator, boy?"

Eli shook his head again.

"Well, they got 'em in New Orleans. Alligators longer than you. I used to catch 'em. Sell they heads to the shops in town for folks to buy. You ain't scared of alligators, is you?"

"No . . . well, kinda," Eli said.

"You don't have to worry none. They can't chew, 'cause they swallow everything whole. All you gotta do is stay out they path. Alligators run fast on land, now. But all you gotta do is run in a zigzag like this." Eli watched the Swamp Man start running from side to side in a crooked line in the clearing. His big coat flapped behind him like wings. Eli started to laugh.

The Swamp Man stopped running.

"Why you don't wanna go to New Orleans?" the Swamp Man asked, breathing hard from all that running.

"'Cause I wanna go see my daddy in Alaska like I been wanting to since way before Ari come to live in our house."

"Your daddy know you coming?"

"No. I'm gonna surprise him."

"Your daddy live up there all by hisself?"

"No, he got a new wife and I got a baby brother."

"You ever seen 'em?"

"Just a picture," Eli said. "I ain't seen my daddy since he moved to Alaska. Talk to him on the phone, though."

"How long ago did he move?"

"When I was five," Eli said sadly.

"That long, huh?" the Swamp Man grunted. "I never did know my daddy. I

know how that kind of missing somebody can feel sometime."

Eli didn't say anything.

"Well," the Swamp Man said, "you
got a long trip ahead of you, boy. Being
a traveling man ain't easy. A traveling
man needs to know how to take care of
hisself. You get cold and hungry sometimes. And it's awfully lonely. You got a
bed at home?"

"Yeah," Eli said.

"Bet it's warm and soft," the Swamp
Man said, stroking his scratchy-looking
chin. He pointed to the shadows under-
neath the bridge.

"That's my bed," he said. He
stretched his arms wide. "This my home.
You welcome to sit with me a minute
and have a bite to eat before you go on
to Alaska."

"You gonna have crawfish?" Eli

asked, and held his breath. He had never been this hungry, but knew he didn't want to eat crawfish. It had to be the same as putting mud inside your mouth.

The Swamp Man laughed like a hyena. He jumped up and down and stomped his feet. He slapped the sides of his coat like he was batting bees away from him.

He wiped the corners of his eyes with his gloves. Finally he chuckled and sputtered and was silent.

"No, boy. We ain't gonna have no crawfish. That all right with you?" he asked.

Eli released the air he had been holding inside his chest. He sounded like a balloon losing air. He gazed into the Swamp Man's watery, blood-streaked eyes. Eyes that had once frightened him terribly now looked so kind.

CHAPTER SEVEN

The Swamp Man bent his lanky body and disappeared under the bridge.

"Come on," he called from the darkness below. Eli went to his bike and slowly wheeled it to the bridge. He stooped and peered into the Swamp Man's home. Piles of blankets and newspapers and scraps of cardboard lay scattered on the ground.

"We can sit on the roof," the Swamp Man said, then chuckled.

Eli straightened and returned to his bike. He pulled Antoine's lucky marble out of the saddlebag. He sat on the edge of the old footbridge's smooth planks, his legs dangling over the side.

Swamp water moved slowly beneath his feet. Sad eyes stared from the mirror of the water.

Eli swung his feet as he rubbed the marble. Maybe Ari was teaching Savannah how to play chess today. He had promised to teach Antoine, Talen, and Jeffre, too. He wouldn't be able to teach Eli if he was in Alaska.

Eli sighed. Now Alaska seemed too far away. If he was home, he could get a glass of lemonade. Instead he might have to drink that old swamp water thick with bugs.

Eli heard the Swamp Man rustling under the bridge.

"Do you want to share some pork and beans?" the Swamp Man asked.

"No, thanks," Eli replied.

"How about some coffee? That's about all I got to drink right now."

"Naw," Eli said, wishing even more he was back at home. He could almost feel his dry fingers holding the slippery iced glass, could almost taste the cool swallow of sweetened lemons sliding down his throat.

The Swamp Man climbed from under the bridge and sat beside Eli, his big boots almost touching the swamp water. He had an open can of pork and beans in his big gloved hands and was eating them with a spoon that could turn into a knife.

"You sure you don't want a bite?" he asked.

Eli took only a second to nod his head. He grabbed the spoon and quickly dipped it inside the can. Beans had never tasted so good. He gobbled several spoonfuls. He lovingly licked the honeyed syrup from the corners of his mouth. Now he was really thirsty.

"Just take a little sip," the Swamp Man said, offering his cup of coffee. "You need something in your throat to help them beans go down."

Eli took a small sip of coffee. The dark-brown liquid tasted bitter on his tongue. He swooshed it around inside his mouth before he finally swallowed. After taking four more sips, he didn't feel quite as thirsty as before.

When the Swamp Man finished eating, he set the empty can on the bridge behind them and took a harmonica out of his pocket.

"We'll see if this don't bring your friend Madison out of his hiding place."

The Swamp Man started to tap his feet in the air, counting one, two, three, and then he started playing. He played a few chords, then stopped.

Eli closed his eyes and for a moment was sitting with his daddy in the rowboat, fishing. While Eli fished, his daddy played the harmonica. He sucked and blew notes that turned into darting bluebirds twirling and prancing over the water and around their glistening fish lines. Eli saw the love gleaming in his daddy's eyes, love shining in his daddy's eyes for him.

"That was one of the songs we sang when we masked Indian in New Orleans," the Swamp Man said.

When the Swamp Man spoke, Eli opened his eyes. Even the Swamp Man's playing couldn't fill the deep hurting space where Eli missed his daddy. But the song helped Eli find the place inside him where he could have his daddy with him, always, even if his daddy was a million miles away.

Then the Swamp Man started singing:

"Shoo fly, don't bother me.
Shoo fly, don't bother me.
Shoo fly, don't bother me,
'Cause I am one of the big chiefs."

The Swamp Man stood and started dance-marching back and forth across the bridge. He looked pretty silly with his big coat flapping. Eli couldn't help but laugh.

"Come on and sing with me," he called out to Eli.

The Swamp Man played his harmonica the same way Eli's daddy used to play, the wiggly sounds turning this way and that inside Eli's head until he felt like those sounds could make him jump out of his skin and fly.

Eli jumped up and started marching behind the Swamp Man, singing:

"Shoo fly, don't bother me.
Shoo fly, don't bother me.
Shoo fly, don't bother me,
'Cause I am one of the big chiefs."

Eli and the Swamp Man marched across the bridge and down to the bank of the swamp. They marched back and forth in the mud looking for Madison. They sang all the while they marched. When Eli got tired of singing, the Swamp Man played his harmonica. Eli almost forgot about Madison and his daddy, Mama, and Savannah, until the Swamp Man blew a screechy note on the harmonica and stopped playing.

The Swamp Man quickly reached down and grabbed something Eli couldn't quite see from a small patch of mucky brown grass.

The Swamp Man gently raised Madison by the tail into the air.

"Got him," the Swamp Man cried. "This old har-monica works every time. Always good for helping folk find things."

He handed Madison to Eli.

"Thanks," Eli said as he carefully cupped Madison inside his hands. He started walking toward the bridge. The Swamp Man followed him.

"Well, I guess you better be on your way if you still want to get to Alaska," the Swamp Man said.

Eli didn't say anything. He walked Madison back to his bike and pulled the silver can out of the saddlebag. He gently placed Madison back inside the can. Eli decided to return Madison to Jeffre before another bad thing could happen to him. He had almost lost him, and he didn't want to lose anything else.

"Maybe I'll just go back home," Eli said. "Maybe I'll go to Alaska some other time."

"Well, I'm sure you got a lot of folk at home who will be awfully glad to see you," the Swamp Man said, and smiled.

Eli couldn't wait to tell Antoine and Talen and Jeffre about the Swamp Man. They had all been wrong. The Swamp Man didn't try to carry him up into the trees or bite his ears. He had only tried to help him. Eli thrust out his hand to shake the Swamp Man's glove. The Swamp Man heartily shook Eli's hand.

"If I go this way to Alaska again, can I stop by and see you?" Eli asked.

"If you go this way, you gotta see me, 'cause this will still be my swamp," the Swamp Man growled.

Eli smiled as he picked up his bike and started walking toward the hill.

"You have a good time when you go to New Orleans. And don't forget to eat some crawfish," the Swamp Man called.

Eli shook his head. He knew he was going to have to go to New Orleans, but he didn't have to eat crawfish. When he had almost reached the bottom of the gravelly hill, he heard the Swamp Man yell, "Catch."

Eli turned and laid his bike on the gravelly ground. The Swamp Man drew back his arm and threw something big and dark at Eli. Eli held up his arms and opened his hands. He grinned as he caught Talen's lucky marble. He put it inside his pants pocket and turned to wave at the Swamp Man, but he was gone.

CHAPTER EIGHT

As Eli pedaled toward home, the main thing on his mind was how happy he would be once Mama put her arms around him. He also couldn't wait to hold a frosty glass of cool lemonade to his lips.

When Eli rode into his driveway, Savannah cartwheeled across the lawn.

"Where have you been, Eli? Ari's looking for you. Mama was worried about you. I wasn't worried though. I told her I hoped you had run away. Did you? Did you try to run away from home?" Savannah asked.

"I been in the woods. With the Swamp Man," Eli calmly replied.

"I have been in the woods," Savannah corrected.

"I didn't see you there," Eli replied.

Savannah made a loud heavy breathing sound like Mama made when she was extra tired.

"Well, Mama called Talen and Miz Ollie said you told Talen something about going to Alaska and Mama called Jeffre's mother, who said she hadn't seen you but then Antoine's father said that Antoine said you were riding your bike to Alaska and Antoine thought maybe he should have gone with you so you wouldn't get caught by a bear or the Swamp Man or something."

"Is Mama mad?" Eli asked.

"You just wait and see." Savannah smirked as she did backflips into the backyard.

Eli wondered how he could have really missed Savannah. He parked his bike inside the garage and slowly walked into the kitchen. J.R. padded softly toward Eli and nudged his leg with his white head. Eli stooped and scooped up the cat. He stroked his sleek gray back.

"Eli!" Mama called.

Eli's heart was pounding inside his chest as loud as Ari beat the table when he practiced for the Indian dance. If Ari were here, he could help Eli make Mama understand. He could tell a joke and make everything all right. But Ari was out looking for Eli, hoping to bring him back home.

Eli ran to Mama and started talking as fast as he could.

"Mama, I rode my bike and played with my new friend at the swamp. He's from Louisiana and eats crawfish and sucks their heads and he used to catch alligators and he masked Indian before like Ari and he thinks I'll have a good time in New Orleans and that I'm lucky to have two dads 'cause he never knew the one he did have and there's black grasshoppers big as Ari's hand in New Orleans and I lost Madison in the swamp grass and all I had to eat was beans and coffee and can I please have a glass of lemonade?" Eli asked.

Eli looked into the mirror of Mama's eyes. He saw his fear there. His fear of being punished, of being lost, of being alone in the world and unloved. He saw that Mama had been afraid for him but was afraid no more. He saw her love for him shining there in her eyes. She smiled at him.

Eli smiled back. Mama was looking at him like suns and moons were in her eyes. Seashells and blue-black stars.

Mama pulled Eli inside her arms and stroked his head.

"Yes, Eli love. You may have a glass of lemonade," she said, and they both laughed, loud and long, there alone in the kitchen.